J.C. HULSEY BOOKS

DOES NORA KNOW?
A Western Short

J.C. HULSEY

Acknowledgement

A very special Thank You to Carl & Kathleen Sutherwood of Carl Sutherwood Photography for allowing the use of their photos on the cover.

West Texas 1875
Garnerville, Renfro County, Texas
It was a little after noon on a Friday. I was really looking forward to a great weekend with Nora. I guess you could call her my fiancé. We've been going together for almost two years and she's always hinting that we should tie the knot.

Lately she's stopped hinting and started insisting. She's one of the finest women I've ever met and she would make a good wife.

I've been the sheriff of this small town for almost five years. I was appointed by the Territorial Judge, who happens to be a very good friend. The judge being a friend was the reason I was one of the youngest sheriffs ever appointed.

Normally the sheriff is elected by the citizens, but this town of Garnerville, Texas was having a hard time locating someone to fill the office, so the judge stepped in and appointed me to the job, along with Harry Clements as my deputy. In this job, I have to travel quite a bit and that's one of the reasons I'm not ready to settle down. Nora doesn't seem to understand my reasoning about this. I can't really blame her. As I said I'm not too thrilled about settling down, but she has been sticking with me through the good and the bad.

~~~~~~

I glanced up from my thoughts and I saw her. Walking down the middle of the street. A little girl, rather small. Not much more than five foot if she was that. As she got closer I saw she was dressed in a plain cotton dress that looked a size too small, and the little bit of hair, sticking out from under her floppy hat, was the color of corn husks. As she came closer, I saw her green eyes, the color of fresh spring grass, was looking at me with a lost puppy look. She looked so mournful, it was all I could do to keep from wrapping my arms around her. But I needed to remember Nora. She was the one who owned my heart. I was only feeling pity for this young girl. Although taking a closer look, the way she fills out that dress tells me she ain't no little girl. Not no more.

"What's your name, Honey?"

She pushed her floppy hat back and looked up at me. "It sure ain't Honey, its Rachel McConnell. What's yours?"
~~~~~~

"Lincoln Rhymes. Where 'bouts you headed, Miss Rachel McConnell? It is Miss, isn't it?"

"'Course it is," she said emphatically. "I ain't never gitting married. I ain't headed no place in particular. Just heading down the road. Wherever it takes me, that's where I'm headed."

"Where you coming from?" I asked.

"You shore ask a lot of questions, even for a law dog," indicating the badge on my vest.

"I asked where you coming from?" ignoring her remark.

"Back yonder a ways," she nodded her head back where she came from.

"Where's back yonder?"

"No place really. I'm trying real hard to forget about there, if you don't mind?"

"I don't reckon I mind. Everybody's got something they want to put behind them."

Just at that moment I heard her stomach growl.

"You want to go get something to eat?" I asked.

"I ain't got no money to buy nothing," she exclaimed.

"How about I buy?"

"I can't let you do that."

"Why not?"

"We ain't been properly introduced," she said. "My mama always told me to stay away from strangers."

"Well, I told you my name and you told me yours. Sounds like we ain't exactly strangers, does it?"

"I reckon you're right," she said shaking her head. "Okay, I'll let you buy me something to eat."

"Great. Follow me."

I walked down the street, with her close behind, to Gold's Eatery. It wasn't the best food, but it was the only eating establishment in town, unless you counted the pickled eggs and slimy sandwiches at the Dew Drop Saloon. We went inside and all the men stopped eating and stared. What they were staring at I didn't know. I turned to tell Rachel to sit and I noticed something I hadn't noticed before. She had removed her hat and that corn husk colored hair was hanging to her shoulders and that too small dress really accentuated her full figure. There was no mistaking her for a little girl now.

I held the chair for her and she seemed surprised by the polite way I treated her.

Leslie Gold, the owner's wife came to the table and asked, "What can I get for you Linc?" she looked at me and then at Rachel.

"We'll have the pork chop special with all the fixings and coffee," I told her. "Bring a pot if you would?"

Leslie returned shortly with plates heaping with food. She set mine down first, then set one in front of Rachel.

"How's Nora," she asked, looking me square in the eye.

"Haven't seen her since last night," I told her spreading the napkin in my lap. "But she was fine then.

"Tell her I said hello," she said, glancing at Rachel, and then back at me. "Next time you see her."

"I'll do that," I said and proceeded to cut up the pork chop on the plate.

Rachel didn't hold back when it came to finishing off her meal. What she lacked in manners, she made up for with enthusiasm. She could put it away with the best of them. She leaned back in her chair and wiped her mouth on her sleeve, completely ignoring the napkin beside her plate.

"That was real good," she said, draining her coffee cup and putting it down. "Now, I reckon you're gonna be wantin' payment for that delicious meal?" She stood up, placed that floppy hat on her head, pushing her hair up under it. "Well, come on."

I stood, told Leslie to put the meal on my tab and followed Rachel out the door. When we got outside, she quickly turned down the alley. I followed.

She turned back toward me and began unbuttoning her dress. "Hold on there!" I said loudly, holding up my hand as if to stop her. "I don't expect any payment from you."

"You'd be the first man I come across that don't want nothing. What's wrong with me? Ain't I pretty enough?" Tears started forming in the corner of her eyes.

"It's not that at all. I bought you a meal because I thought you were hungry. I don't expect anything in return other than your friendship."

"That's what I was trying to do," she sniffed. "Be friendly. So you're telling me you don't want nothing from me, but being my friend?"

"That's exactly what I mean. Now, I asked you before, where were you going? You really didn't give a definitive answer."

"A defin . . . what?"

"You didn't tell me where you were going."

"Oh. It's like I told you. I ain't got no place in particular to go. I just go from town to town trying to get a job. Ain't nobody wants to hire a girl, so, I just head on to the next town."

"How old are you?" I asked her.

"Almost eighteen, in a couple months. Why?"

"Where's your folks? How come they let you go traipsing around the country, like this?"

"Ain't nobody 'septin' my step daddy and he was always trying to do things he shouldn't, so I skid daddled outta there. Ain't looked back neither," she said proudly.

"Where's your ma? I asked her.

"Sinclair killed her, that's my step daddy," she said shaking her head. "Oh, the law said they didn't have no proof, but he done it. I know he did. He'd probably killed me if I hadn't got outta there."

"You got any brothers or sisters?" I asked.

"Got a step brother. He's another reason I left. He's been trying to fool around with me for a couple of years. One thing my mama told me when she was alive was to not let nobody mess with me less'en I wanted'em to."

"Sounds like you done the right thing getting outta there," I told her. "Say? Wait a minute? You said Sinclair?"

"Yeah. Why?"

"There was a Sinclair McConnell killed a couple months back. They said the law went to talk to him about rustling some cows. He had one of them cows strung up in the barn butchering it. When they tried to take him in, he rushed at the deputy with the skinning knife and the sheriff shot him dead," I told her. "You're not gonna have to worry no more about him."

"What 'bout Donnie?" she asked. "Did he git killed too?"

"Didn't hear nothing about no Donnie. He your stepbrother?"

"Yeah, wish they'd shot him too. Good riddance to'em both."

"You got any money? Any more clothes than what you're wearing?" I noticed she wasn't carrying a sack or anything. I scanned the street in both directions as if I thought somebody was watching us.

She shook her head. "Nope. What you see is what you get. Why you asking all these questions?" she looked at me quizzically.

"I want to help you," I told her. "Without any obligations, I might add."

"There you go with them big words again. Why cain't you talk English?" she said, shaking her head.

"I want to help you without you feeling like you have to pay me or give me something in return," I explained. "There. Is that plain enough for you?"

"I don't understand?" she said, shaking her head again.

"What don't you understand?" I asked her.

"I ain't never had nobody do something just 'cause they want to."

"Well, you have now and the first thing we're going to do is get you a bath and then some clothes." I told her.

"Why do I need a bath? You think I'm dirty?" she almost cried.

"I think you're a lovely young woman that will be even lovelier when you have a bath and new clothes. Now comeon." I offered her my arm.

She looked at it as if she didn't know what to do. I took her hand, placed it in the crook of my arm and we started walking. I glanced down and saw she had a big smile plastered on her lovely face. I had told her she was lovely and I didn't lie.

~~~~~~

We walked to the barber shop and went in. "Hello Linc," said Thaddeus Hunsaker, the barber as he eyeballed Rachel.

"Hello, Thad, you got a tub filled with water back there?" nodding toward the back.

"Yeah, I'll just have to heat a couple buckets, then it'll be ready. You gonna take a bath in the middle of the day?" he asked.

"It ain't for me. It's for the young lady." I nodded to Rachel.
~~~~~~

"I don't know as I can allow a female to take a bath in my establishment," he said frowning and shaking his head. "What if someone comes in wanting a bath, like a man?"

"You can ask them to wait, can't you?" I handed him a twenty dollar gold piece.

"Of course," as he stuck the coin in his pocket. "It's all yours. Or in this case yours, ma'am. Enjoy your bath. I'll be right back with the hot water," he rushed from the room.

"You want me to take a bath in a men's bath house?" she asked me.

"Let's say it's a girl's bath house today. You go on in and get in the tub. I'm going to the general store and pick out some clothes for you. I'll be back, so don't leave the premises."

"You and all them big words," she said, shaking her head as she went through the curtain to the back room.

"Don't leave here until I get back, okay?" I hollered as she went through the curtain. "Thad?" I yelled.

"Yeah!" he answered.

"I'm leaving for a bit. I expect you to protect the young woman if the need arises."

"Okay, don't worry about a thing. I'll watch her like she was my own daughter."

I left the barber shop and went to the general store.

~~~~~~

"Hello, Linc," the owner, Wilford Watkins, said as I entered.

"Hi, Will. I need some things that perhaps your wife might be better suited to help me," I asked looking around the store.

"Is she here?"

"Florence? Somebody needs your help," he called. "She'll be right out. What on earth could you need that I couldn't help you?" looking quizzically at me.

"You can listen as I explain to Flo. If you want to?" I told him.

"Oh, how are you Linc?" asked Florence when she appeared from behind the curtain. "What can I help you with? Something for Nora, I presume?"

"No, not this time," I said. "However, I am needing a couple of dresses with all the paraphernalia that goes
~~~~~~

with them for a young woman about this high," I indicated holding my hand almost even with my chest. She not too fleshy, but she ain't skinny neither," I explained to her.

Florence's eyes shot up as she contemplated whether she was going to question me about this situation. She decided the negative. "Is there any particular color you want?" she asked, walking toward a rack holding dresses.

"I think that yellow one there and the blue one will fill the bill. You know better than me the other stuff she needs." I told her and turned to visit with Thad.

"What you got going on?" he asked and leaned across the counter as if I had a secret only for his ears. "Does Nora know about all this?"

"No, she does not, and I would appreciate it if you and Flo didn't mention it just yet," I told him. "I want to be the one to tell her."

"Here you are, Linc," said Flo as she placed a stack of things on the counter. I believe this is everything a young woman will need. You did say she was young, didn't you?" she raised her eyebrows in a questioning look. "Does Nora know about this . . . situation?"

"No, and I've already warned your husband that I wanted to be the one to tell her," I looked first at Thad and then at Flo. "Do you both understand?"

They both shook their heads.

"I would like to hear the words, if it's not too much trouble."

"Yes, Lincoln, we understand. You want to tell Noreen yourself, therefore we are not to say anything to anyone."

"How much do I owe you?" I asked reaching for my purse.

"Looks like it adds up to an even twelve dollars," said Thad.

I gave him a double eagle and said, "Keep the change." I picked up the packages, tucked them under my arm, nodded to the couple and left the building.

~~~~~~

I went back to the barber shop and neither Thad nor Rachel were in the front room. I heard a commotion in the back. I pushed the curtain aside and almost got plastered in the face with a wet rag flying through the air.

"Whoa!" I yelled. "What's going on?"
~~~~~~

"Thank goodness, you're here," said Thad excitedly. "I can't get the girl outta the tub. She's been in there ever since you left. She's gonna turn into a prune before long."

"Alright, Thad, you go on. I'll take care of it," I motioned for him to leave.

"Rachel," I said calmly as I walked over to the tub. I shouldn't have gotten so close because all the soap bubbles had dissipated and I could see almost all the way to the bottom of the tub. But I didn't see the bottom because it was blocked by other things that I shouldn't be looking at. I quickly averted my eyes and said, "Rachel, Honey, you need to consider getting out of the tub. I think you've soaked enough today," I used my pleading voice.

"I thought we done decided my name ain't Honey!" she said loudly.

"I'm sorry, Rachel," I said with my guilty voice. "Would you please get out of the tub? There are others wanting to take a bath. We'll plan on doing this again real soon. How's that sound?"

"Oh, alright. First, you want me in the tub, then you want me outta the tub. I shore wish you could decide what you want," she stood splashing water all over me.

"Hand me that towel, I can't reach it," she said tapping my wet shoulder.

I handed her the towel and stepped away with my back turned to her.

"Did you git me some new clothes, like you said?" she asked. "I shore would hate to put that dirty dress back on after spending so much time gitting cleaned up."

"I got you some," I said. "I'm gonna step out in the front room while you dress. Call me if you need help with the buttons," which I hoped she didn't.

~~~~~~

"Where did you pick up that wildcat?" asked Thad as I came through the curtain.

"I don't think she's all that bad," I said in her defense.

"You wasn't here when I asked her nicely, mind you," he said, "that she should get out of the tub. I ain't never heard a mule skinner use some of the words that came outta that girl's mouth."
~~~~~~

"You talking 'bout me, are you?" we both turned to the sound of her voice. I heard Thad take a deep breath. I was afraid if I did, I might not get it back.

Rachel was beautiful. She had pulled her still wet hair back in a ponytail and was wearing the pale blue dress which both flattered her and was a perfect fit.

"Well, if you gentlemen will close your mouth and tell me how I look, I would appreciate it," she said turning in a circle.

Thad looked at me and I looked at him, both of us shaking our heads in disbelief.

"Does Nora know about her?" asked Thad.

I didn't answer. *Who was Nora?* That's the thought that was going through my mind.

"Now that I'm all prettified, what's next," she batted her eyelashes at me and I felt my heart skip a beat.

I cleared my throat and said, "We need to get you a room at the hotel."

"I ain't never been in a hotel before. What's it like?" Again with the fluttering eyelids.

"Instead of me trying to explain," I said offering my arm. "Why don't we go see?"

She was a quick learner, because this time she slipped her arm through mine and started leading me out of the barber shop.

"Good luck," Thad called and turned away to go clean up the spilled water in the bathing room.

I will admit, it gave me a good feeling to have this young lady walking beside me. What was it that was different about her that made me want to forget Nora? Something I couldn't put my finger on and something I shouldn't be doing.

~~~~~~

We walked into the hotel lobby and the two men that were sitting there talking became very quiet and turned so they could see us clearly. The desk clerk, a scrawny, pipsqueak of a man that I had never cared for, came to attention when he saw me, then his eyes turned to Rachel. I saw him blink and heard him swallow. He glanced back at me, then back at her. "What can I do for you, Sheriff?" he asked without looking at me.

"I'd like a room, please?" tapping the desk with a coin.
~~~~~~

He jerked his eyes away from Rachel and said all business like, "A single or a double?" he winked with that pimply face and his greasy slicked down hair. It was too much for me to take.

I reached across the desk, grabbed the front of his shirt and jerked him across the desk. "I want you to put your dirty mind back to sleep, where it needs to stay, for the remainder of Miss McConnell's visit to your establishment. Do you understand me?" I shoved him back.

He struggled to stay on his feet and tried to adjust his rumbled shirt. "Yes sir, Sheriff Rhymes, Only the best for Miss McConnell. Room six, top of the stairs, hallway on the left. I apologize if I offended you, Miss McConnell," he slid the key across the desk and stepped back.

I picked it up along with the packages from the store and held out my arm again. We walked side by side up the stairs, turned left and walked down the hall to room number six.

"This is yours, Miss McConnell," and handed her the key.

"You open it, please," again with the fluttering eyelashes. Handing the key back to me.

I took it, inserted it in the lock, glancing at her. I could see the excitement in her face and eyes. She looked like a kid opening toys on Christmas morning.

I twisted the key, hearing the lock as it flipped the tumbler, turned the knob and pushed the door open. I stepped back and indicated she should enter.

She stepped over the threshold and I heard an audible gasp from her as she tried to suppress a cry. She ran to the bed and sat on the edge, then she lay back on it and flapped her arms as if making a snow angel.

"She sat up, looked at me with those green eyes, the color of fresh spring grass and that lost puppy look. The same look she'd had when I first saw her. I could feel those eyes drawing me into her world.

What's wrong with you? You can't be having these kind of thoughts. You'll be marrying Nora in a short time. "I'm gonna leave now," I stammered. "If you need anything, tell that idiot at the desk. He'll get a message to me."

"Do you really have to leave?" *Those damn eyes are going to be the death of me.* I quickly looked away from her and said, "Yes, I have some other things to take care of. Like I said, if you need anything, tell the clerk to send me a message. I'll come by in the morning and we'll have breakfast. Good bye." I turned and left, pulling the door closed behind me. I stopped and leaned against it taking a deep breath. I had never in all my born days felt this attracted to any woman. Not even Nora.

I straightened up, took a deep breath and went down the stairs. I stopped and explained to the clerk what was expected of him. He nodded his head that he understood.

I gave him a coin and left the building. The two gentlemen that were sitting there, when we came in, now had their heads together whispering and looking my way. I tipped my hat to them on my way out.

What was I going to tell Nora about Rachel? Did I have to tell her? I need to tell her, don't I? Does she really need to know? I'll send Rachel on her way tomorrow and Nora will never know anything about her.

Nora lives in a little brown house on the end of Faraday Street. She's part owner of the dress shop in town. This was a slow time of the year for dresses, with it being harvest time.

After all the crops were gathered and sold, then the ladies would be wanting new clothes.

I hoped she had supper ready. I was just a little on the hungry side. I hadn't eaten since the meal I shared with

Rachel. Which reminds me, she hasn't eaten since then either.

Don't be thinking about her when you're on your way to Nora's house. I had almost reached the front of her house when I heard my name called. I stopped and turned toward the sound. *Oh no! It's Rachel.*

~~~~~~

"Rachel, what are you doing here?" I asked, looking toward Nora's house half expecting her to come running out the door accusing me, of what, I don't know.

"I was gittin' hungry and since I don't have no money to git nothing," she explained, "I didn't know what else to do, but look for you. You've been so nice to me and I knew if anybody would help me, you would."

"Why didn't you send the clerk for me?" I asked her.
~~~~~~

"He was asleep and when I woke him he told me where to find you. Did I do something wrong?" she asked. "You seem upset."

"No, I'm not upset. In fact, I'm hungry too. What do you say we go get a big steak with all the fixings?"

"That sounds delicious," she said, slipping her arm in mine.

I looked back at Nora's house secretly hoping she wouldn't come out the door or look through a window.

Rachel talked and talked all the way to the eatery. I only heard bits and pieces of what she said. My mind was engaged in a wrestling match with itself. What to do about Nora. I need to let Rachel know about Nora, so there'll be no misunderstanding later on.

We reached the eatery and went inside. I thought everyone stared the first time we came in here, but this time, the only thing I could hear was my own heartbeat.

"It sure got awful quiet, didn't it?" Rachel asked.

"Yeah, that's what happens when a pretty girl walks into a place," I told her and held the chair for her.

"I don't see no pretty girl," she said looking all around. "Where is she?" she didn't realize how pretty she was.

Leslie came over, "Hello again, Linc. Two times in one day. That's unusual, isn't it?" she said looking at Rachel. "Why, you're the same girl that was in here earlier. You look very nice," she turned back to me. "What'll it be?" pulling a pad from her apron.

"We'll have two steaks with all the stuff that comes with them," I told her.

"You want coffee or tea?" Leslie asked, placing the pad back in her apron pocket.

I looked at Rachel and she said, "I ain't never had tea before. Can I git that?" How could I refuse anything for this beautiful young woman that seemingly had me under some kind of spell?

"We'll have tea," I told Leslie.

"Coming right up," she said as she turned and hurried away.

"I been meaning to ask you," said Rachel. "Who is Nora? Is she your girlfriend or something?"

"She's . . . "I hesitated. Why I hesitated, I can't tell you, but I did. Why couldn't I just spit it out? Tell Rachel I'm the same as engaged to be married. Somehow, I didn't want her to know. I didn't want to end this relationship, if that's what it is with Rachel. Not yet, maybe not ever. I opened my mouth to try to explain when the meal came.

Then we were too busy eating to continue talking, of which I was glad.

When Rachel started to wipe her mouth with her sleeve, the dress didn't have any sleeves.

"If I may?" I reached and handed her the folded napkin beside her plate. "Use this, it's the way a lady wipes her mouth."

She took the napkin, looked at it as if it was some creature that was going to harm her, then she touched it to her mouth, dabbing a little just like a high society lady. She was indeed a fast learner.

She lay the napkin down and grinned at me, again batting those hypnotizing eyelashes at me, causing the food I had in my mouth to go down the wrong way. I started coughing, trying to clear my throat.

"Are you alright?" she asked, placing her tiny hand on my arm. I jerked it back as her touch felt like a hot branding iron on my skin. This girl was like a stick of dynamite ready to explode. And it looked as though I was going to be the recipient of that explosion.

"Are you finished?" I asked her wiping my mouth and pushing my plate back.

"Yes, I'm done, and I might say that was very good. Thank you kind sir for your generosity. How's that for one of your big words?" she asked with a big grin on her lovely face.

"I have to admit, you surprised me, all right."

"My mama did teach me a few things," she said. "But I just about forgot'em."

"I'm sure they'll all come back to you," I stood, indicating I was ready to leave. I walked to the front counter to pay Leslie while Rachel waited by the door.

"Ain't none of my business, Linc," she said quietly. "But does Nora know about this?" she nodded her head in Rachel's direction.

"Like you said, it ain't none of your business, but I'm

gonna tell you. No. Nora doesn't know. Yet! And I would appreciate it if you would let me be the one to tell her. Can you do that for me, please?" I asked her.

"Of course, Linc. Like I said, it really ain't none of my business. Here's your change," handing me back a handful of coins, which I stuck in my pocket.

I nodded to her, turned and walked over to Rachel. Once more I was amazed at how beautiful she looked. Apparently I wasn't the only one affected. Every eye in the room was turned toward us as we left.

~~~~~~

We walked back to the hotel and was about to enter, when I heard someone call my name. We stopped and turned to see Harrison Clements running across the street. Harry is my deputy, partner, and friend, also appointed by the territorial Judge, same as me.

"I been looking all over town fer you. This message jest came over the wire. Says there was a bank robbery in Lynix County."

"Okay, you found me, take a deep breath while I get Rachel settled in here. By the way, Rachel, this is my associate, Harrison Clements. Harry, this is Rachel, she's
~~~~~~

. . . a friend." *There goes that hesitation again.* "Rachel," I said looking into those eyes again. I looked back at Harry, then back at Rachel without looking directly at her face. "Can you find your way to your room? I have a matter to attend to. I'll see you tomorrow."

"Yes, of course I can find my way to my room, I'm not some little kid that needs her hand held every minute," she fussed at me, then turned to Harry. "It was a pleasure to meet you Mr. Clements." With that, she turned and entered the hotel.

"Don't say it?" I said to Harry warningly.

"Say what," he looked innocently at me. "I wasn't gonna say nothing. But I was wondering."

"Don't wonder neither," I warned him. "Tell me about this job."

"Here," he handed me the telegram. I opened it and read.

The bank in Lynix County was robbed by the notorious Fletcher gang led by Luther Fletcher. Fletcher has a reputation as a vicious killer. The telegram stated that he had gunned down the bank teller and then on the way out of town he had shot and killed the sheriff, then as he reached the end of town, he turned in the saddle and laughed when he shot a young boy who just wanted to take a look at a real bank robber.

The doctor doesn't give much hope of the boy surviving.

Your job is to hunt them down, apprehend them and bring them back for a trial.

Harry said what he always said. "Why we got to bring'em in. They're just gonna hang anyway. Let's save the town a lot of trouble and put these hombres out of their misery."

"Now Harry, you know that ain't the way the law works. There's a certain procedure that has to be followed."

"Yeah, I know, rules and regulations and all that nonsense."

"That's right. Now quit your fussing and let's go after these guys."

We were just about ready to leave town when Ben Strange, the telegraph operator came running up the street hollering, "Hold up, Linc, I got another wire here for you."

"What's it say," I asked him wanting to get moving.

"It says they done captured the Fletcher gang. So I reckon you don't have to leave after all."

"Boy, that's a load off my shoulders," said Harry. "I shore was dreading tangling with them yahoos."

"Don't get too comfortable just yet, Harry," said Ben.

"There's another wire here telling about a mean one headed this'a way."

"Give it to me," I dismounted. "Take my horse back to the livery stable, will you, Harry?"

"Sure thing, Boss."

"You know I don't like it when you call me that."

"Yeah, I know," he took the reins from me and rode toward the livery stable.

"Thanks," I told Ben. I opened the message and read.

Donnie McConnell headed your direction. Wanted for bank robbery and murdering the teller and the bank president in Jackson County. He also gunned down an old man who was just sitting in front of the feed store minding his own business. Consider him to be extremely dangerous.

Signed Kendrick Grayson – Acting Sheriff.

Harry came walking up, coming from the stable. "What's it say?"

"That name sounds familiar. McConnell!" I scratched my head. "That's Rachel's step brother."

"You mean that sweet looking young thing has got a killer for kin?" asked Harry.

"Let's keep this between us for right now," I told him.

"You better go inform Ben not to spread it around until you tell him different."

"I'll remind him it's a federal offense to reveal the contents of a telegram to anyone other than it's addressed."

"He already knows that I know, but he is a human being and we all know they make mistakes."

~~~~~~

"What you gonna do, while I'm doing that?"

"I think I better talk to Rachel and try to get more information on her stepbrother."

"I think I like my job better," said Harry.

"I'm not looking forward to it," I told him.

He headed one direction and I headed for the hotel. I was relieved to find the lobby empty and the desk clerk
~~~~~~

wasn't behind the desk. It wouldn't be doing anybody any good to see me going to Rachel's room this late at night.

I took the stairs two at a time, reached her door and knocked softly. I removed my hat, pressed my ear to the wood and didn't hear anything. I knocked a little louder.

"Okay, okay, I'm coming. Hold your horses," she heard me that time. The door swung open and standing there before me in just her chemise was an angel.

I quickly regained my composure and scolded her, "Don't you know better than to open the door before you know who it is?"

"I knew it was either you, your friend Harry or that greasy haired desk clerk. I knew you or Harry wouldn't do nothing and if that pipsqueak from downstairs tried anything, I'd knock him on his ear. "You gonna come in or stand out in the hall all night?" I stepped into the room and heard the door close behind me.

"What is it you want?" she asked, stifling a yawn with her tiny hand. Her beautiful hand. "I was fast asleep having a wonderful dream. I shore hope it's important. I want to get back in that dream if I can."

"I need to ask you about Donnie, your stepbrother."

"I done told you about him. He's sorry and no account. They shoulda kilt him when they kilt Sinclair. Oh I reckon there's a few good memories with him, but . . . Say, why you asking about him?"

"I just got word that he's coming here."

"Is he looking for me?" she asked with a quivering voice.

"I don't think he is, but he could be. I just wanted to let you know so's you could watch out for him. Don't go off no place by yourself. Stay close to town. If you need anything you send that jerk downstairs for me. Don't go no place alone."

"I kin take care of myself. You don't got no need to worry."

"But I will. I do worry about you," I took her hand in mine. "I don't think I could stand it if something happened to you."

"You really feel that way about me?" squeezing my hand.

"I think I do," looking into those hypnotizing green eyes.

"I don't know when or how it happened, but I think I might be in love with you. Hellfire, there ain't no might about it. I do love you."

"Oh Linc," she put her arms around my neck. "I love you too. I think I loved you the moment I first laid eyes on you.

Now kiss me."

I removed her hands from my neck and stepped back.

"There is one thing though," I said, hanging my head.

"What?" she asked with that lost puppy look. "Tell me."

"There's Nora."

"Yeah, you never did tell me who Nora is."

"Nora's my fiancé," I told her twisting my hat in my hand. "We're supposed to get married any day now."

"I thought you just told me you loved me?" she said, tears forming in the corner of her eyes.

"I did," I said quickly. "But I can't hurt Nora. I've got to find an easy way to tell her without hurting her. You can understand that, can't you?"

"I'm afraid I don't really understand, but one thing."

"What's that?" I asked.

"I understand that you love me and I love you," she said as she turned her back to me. "I don't understand why it should involve anybody else. If this Nora is a nice person, which I know she is or she wouldn't have been sweet on you. If she's nice, she'll understand and step aside so you and me can be happy."

I reached and turned her back around to face me, took her hand in mine and said, "Yes, Nora is a fine woman. She's a nice decent woman, but she and I have been seeing each other for quite a while." I tossed my hat aside and took her other hand. "Because she is all these things, I don't want to hurt her. What if things were switched around and it was you in Nora's place? What would you want me to do?"

She turned her face up to look at me, tears sliding down her cheeks, "Since you put it that way, I reckon I understand a little, but let me tell you this," she pulled her hands free. "If it was the other way around, I wouldn't let you go without a fight. If I had to scratch her eyes out, I would fight to keep you."

"That's exactly the reason I have to convince Nora that I don't love her anymore. That I love you and I want to spend the rest of my life with you," I looked at her, my heart thumping in my chest. "I'd rather face a mountain lion or a grizzly bear than to face Nora with this."

"Could you do me a favor before you leave?" she asked.

"Sure, what is it?"

"Kiss me and let me feel how much you love me," she begged with those green eyes.

I took her in my arms. A tiny woman's body, but a grown woman's body. I tilted her face up and I lowered mine until our lips barely touched. She placed her arms around my neck, pulling my lips against hers. The moment she pressed her lips against mine, it was like I was transformed into another world, another realm of reality. I had never felt anything like this in my entire life. Lips as smooth as velvet, tasting like the sweetest honey ever produced by a swarm of bees. I could feel the passion building as we stood there with our lips together.

I reached up and untangled her arms from my neck and stepped back. I was breathing hard, my heart felt as if it was going to jump outta my chest. I looked at Rachel.

Her eyes were still closed, then she opened them, fire flashing from them.

She spoke with a venom in her voice, "You go see this woman named Nora, and you tell her that I'll fight the devil himself to keep you. I will not give you up, so she better be a nice little girl and step aside, or else. You tell her that. And Linc?"

"Yes?"

"Remember this, above everything else, I LOVE YOU!

Now go get some sleep and first thing in the morning, you go see your ex finance." She stood on tip toes and gave me a peck on my cheek.

~~~~~~

I grabbed my hat from the bed where I had tossed it earlier and left her room, feeling extremely content. More so than I ever had. Then reality set in. Not only did I have Nora to contend with, but Donnie McConnell was heading this direction and he could be trouble. Big trouble.

Harry was waiting on the steps of the hotel, "Did you learn anything worthwhile?"
~~~~~~

"Oh yes, I learned something worthwhile." I said with a big smile.

"What did she say?"

"She said she loves me."

"Huh?" asked Harry. "Didn't you ask about her stepbrother? I thought that's what you went to see her about."

"She don't know any more about him than he's a mean person and she wishes he had been killed when her step-daddy was killed."

"Now, what's all this love stuff? You forget about Nora? You two are engaged and are supposed to be married any time. You didn't forget, did you?"

"No, I didn't forget about Nora, but something happened, Harry. I didn't mean for it to happen. I didn't plan it, but it happened just the same," I took my hat off and rubbed my hand through my hair. "I love her, Harry. I don't think I've ever felt this way about anyone before, not even Nora."

"What are you gonna tell Nora?" he asked, shaking his head. "You know she's been planning this wedding for a spell now."

"Well, right now, we need to try to get a few hours of rest. Let's go home and give it a try." Home being a small one room cabin in back of the jail. Sheriff's quarters is what the council called it. They weren't very happy about the judge stepping in and appointing me and Harry to the job.

We walked home and went inside. I removed my gunbelt. "It sure ain't fancy, is it?" I said to Harry.

"Don't need fancy when you're asleep." he said. "I sleep with my eyes closed, can't see whether it's fancy or not." He flopped down on the thin mattress. "Ouch! Goodnight."

"Good night, Harry." I sat on the edge of the bunk and placed my face in my hands. Finally, after a few thoughts, I laid down and closed my eyes. Sleep didn't come easy that night, but I finally drifted off, only to be awakened in what seemed a couple of seconds.

"Rise and shine Romeo," he teased. "Let's go git some breakfast and then make a plan for this Donnie McConnell they say is headed our way."

We made our way to Gold's Eatery and ordered a big breakfast of eggs, bacon, johnny cakes and a pot of black coffee.

When Leslie came back to refill the coffee pot, she said, "Nora was here before I even opened the door this morning. She was asking about you and that girl. Don't worry, I remembered what you told me as how you wanted to be the one to tell her, so God forgive me, I lied. You hear me, Linc? I lied to Noreen, one of my friends, because I didn't want to hurt her."

"I'm sorry I put you in that situation, Leslie. I'm gonna go see her as soon as I can and explain everything to her. Thanks for not telling her."

"I didn't do it for you, Lincoln Rhymes. I did it for her. I couldn't stand to see her hurt. You better tell her real soon before someone else spills the beans." She turned and walked away.

"Boy, you shore know how to stir up things, don't you?" commented Harry.

"I can't face either one of them until this trouble with Donnie McConnell is over and done with. I've got to concentrate on that and not let these others things distract me. If you're finished, let's go back to the office and make some plans." I stood, turned my cup up and drained it, then placed it back on the table.

Harry did the same, then stood and said, "Let's git'er done."

I waved to Leslie as we left, she nodded and proceeded to take an order from some folks that had just come in.

Harry and I were walking slowly back to the jail when I glanced up and saw a sorry looking sorrel horse coming round the corner of the last building at the end of the street. It was too far away to make out who was riding it, but I had a feeling it was Donnie.

"Take a gander," I told Harry and pointed down the street.

"Think that might be him?" he asked, placing his hand on his weapon.

"Don't know yet, but let's step to the side outta sight and see if he comes this way." We both dropped behind the corner of the feed store and watched as the horse and rider drew closer. When he got close enough for us to see the rider's face,

Harry exclaimed, "It ain't nobody but old man Taylor. What's he doing in town today? He don't never come in but once a month."

"Wish I knew what this McConnell fellow looks like," I said to Harry. "It would sure be easier on my nerves."

"I know exactly what you mean."

We stepped out from our hiding place and Old man Taylor hollered. "Hold on, Sheriff! I's on my way to yer office. You saved me the trouble," he slid off the back of his horse and walked over to us.

"What can I do for you, Mr. Taylor?" I asked.

"First thing you kin do is quit calling me mister. You and Harry both know I don't like it, not one bit."

"I apologize, Jethro," I held up my hands in mock surrender. "What are you needing this morning?"

"Got a message fer you," he hesitated like he was waiting for me to ask what message, so I did.

"What message do you have for me?"

"A young feller came in to my place around midnight. Told me he was hungry and could I give him somethin' to eat. Well, I fixed him some scrambled eggs. That's when he told me. Mind you, he told me. He didn't ask, if you know what I mean. He told me to come into town and tell the sheriff, he better send his sister out there or there's gonna be hellfire and brimstone falling down on this town. Let me tell you, I was really glad to git away from that feller," he shook his head and continued talking. "Them green eyes of his seemed to turn black when he told me, I better hurry, if I knew what was good fer me. I'm an old man and I seen a lot of things in my life, but I ain't never seen a man's eyes change color like that. That man's got the devil inside him."

"Thanks, Jethro, here's a dollar," I pressed a coin in his hand. "Go over to Gold's and have a breakfast on the sheriff's office. Thanks again for the information."

He grabbed that coin like he thought it was gonna fly away before he got a hold on it, nodded his head, turned and led his horse toward the eatery.

"We gonna go out there and face him?" asked Harry.

"That would probably be best. I don't want him coming to town and hurting any innocent folks."

"You believe all that stuff Jethro said 'bout his eyes changing color and all?"

"Worse things than that have been reported happening. When you're dealing with a crazy person, you should always be prepared for anything, even seemingly impossible things."

"You shore ain't making me feel no better about going out there."

We walked to the livery stable to get our mounts. Albert Hawks, the hostler was just walking outta the tack room, pulling up his suspenders over dirty long johns.

"Morning fellers," he said while yawning. "Yer here mighty early. You wanting yer horses, are you?"

"Yes, we got to go outta town," fussed Harry. "And it's a lot easier on horseback."

"What's got Harry riled up this morning?" Hawks looked at me.

I just shrugged my shoulders and answered, "I hadn't noticed."

Hawks disappeared out the back door and returned shortly with our horses. "Where 'bouts you headed outta town?" he looked at me, then at Harry.

"We're goin' to see the devil himself," exclaimed Harry as he mounted and lit out toward Jethro's place.

"We're going out to Jethro Taylor's place. If we're not back by, say two o'clock, you better send somebody to check on us, but tell'em to be mighty cautious."

"Sure thing, Linc. You be careful yourself."

I mounted my horse, turned him in the direction Harry had gone, gave him a little kick in the ribs and we took off at a gallop.

~~~~~~

It was a good two hour ride to Taylor's farm. We stopped on a little rise before we went down to the house.

"How you want to play this?" asked Harry.

"You try to work your way around the back of the house. I'm gonna ride right up to the front door, dismount, walk up and knock on the door."

"You're taking an awful risk doing that, don't you think?"

"Not if I take my badge off. Maybe he'll think I'm just visiting old man Taylor. At least I hope so. Go ahead, I'll give you a good five minutes, and then I'll ride on down."

Harry climbed off his horse, tied the reins to a low hanging branch and started off through the bushes.
~~~~~~

I removed my badge and stuck it in my shirt pocket. All of a sudden, I started sweating and my heart started racing. I don't reckon I'll ever be able to do this sort of thing without getting nervous. I said a silent prayer for the Lord to watch over Harry and me. I've never been much for praying, but I felt that this was as good a time as any to give it a try.

When I felt five minutes had passed, I pointed my horse downhill to the Taylor farm house. The closer I got, it seemed my heart slowed down a little and I felt a calmness slip over me.

I stopped about five feet from the front door and hollered, "Hello, Mr. Taylor! You in there?" Of course he wasn't. He was in town waiting for us to move this character out of his house. I dismounted and walked up to the door. I had just raised my hand to knock when it was jerked open and I was staring down the barrel of a rifle.

"What'd you want here, Mister?" the man asked. "There ain't no Mr. Taylor here. He sold this place to me and left the country."

I quickly stuck my hands in the air. "I don't mean to disturb you, but Mr. Taylor didn't say anything about selling out and moving on. I just talked to him yesterday. Could you please point that rifle somewhere else, please?" I still had my hands in the air.

He lowered the weapon. "You need to move on out, I don't want no visitors. I done told you Mr. Taylor ain't here."

"Okay, but maybe you could give me a cup of coffee. Mr. Taylor always gave me a cup of coffee, seeing as how we're neighbors and all," I told him stepping inside the door. "Now that you and me are neighbors, we could get better acquainted over a cup of coffee." I pushed the door closed with my boot as I still had my hands in the air.

"I reckon since we're neighbors," he said. "I could spare a cup of joe."

"Okay if I put my hands down, neighbor?" slowly lowering my hands.

"Sure, I reckon that'll be alright. Sit there at the table. I got a pot here on the stove." He laid the rifle across the table and turned his back on me to get the pot off the stove.

This kid was green as a newborn calf. I grabbed the rifle, stood and said, "Donnie McConnell, you're under arrest."

He froze for a second, then grabbed the hot coffee pot and twirled throwing the hot boiling liquid in my direction. I was lucky enough to duck and only a little of the scalding liquid got on my shoulder.

Donnie took that moment of me being distracted to run out the back door and smack into Harry. "Where 'bouts you think you're going young feller?" Harry asked as he poked his six shooter in Donnie's gut.

"You okay in there, Linc?" Harry shouted.

"I'm okay, be there in a second and slap the cuffs on our young friend."

"No hurry, he ain't going no place, not without any lead in him."

I wiped some lard on the burned places on my shoulder, then went outside with Harry and the prisoner.

I had Donnie put his hands behind his back and I fastened the cuffs on rather tight.

"Ouch!" he complained. "That hurts."

"You'll live," I told him. "Which is more than I can say about those folks you killed."

"You're talking crazy," he growled. "I didn't kill nobody, you don't know what you're talking about."

"I've got a telegram in my pocket says different," I told him and patted my shirt pocket where the paper was tucked away. "You can plead your innocence to a judge and jury. If you convince them you're innocent, then you can go free. Come on, let's go back to town."

"I can't ride like this?" Donnie fussed. "With my hands behind my back."

"We'll help you in the saddle," I told him. "I believe you'll survive the trip."

"But," said Harry. "If you happen to fall off your horse and break your neck, it'll save the town the cost of a trail."

We arrived back in town just as the sun was disappearing over the horizon. We pulled up and stopped in front of the jail. Harry and I got off, but Donnie stayed in the saddle.

"You're gonna have to help me to the saddle, Lawdog," he snarled.

"Okay," said Harry reaching up, grabbing him by the collar and jerking him onto the ground. "Oh, I'm sorry, did you hurt yourself?" he jerked him upright and started guiding him through the door and into a cell.

"You gonna take these cuffs off now," whined Donnie. "I can't feel my hands no more, there're so tight."

"All in good time. Why don't you just rest yourself on the bunk there?" I told him. "We'll be back shortly."

"You're being downright cruel," whined Donnie. "Ain't there a law against that?"

"Son," I turned and glared at him, "I am the law and what I say and do will stand. Come on, Harry, let's go." We turned and left Donnie McConnell whining and crying in that cell.

"He shore was a lot easier than I thought. I never did see his eyes change color neither," said Harry.

"Kid's very green," shaking my head. "He laid his rifle right on the table in front of me, then turned his back. "It's like he wanted to get caught."

Let's get a little sleep, then in the morning, I've got to go see Nora."

"I don't envy you that little chore," Harry said shaking his head. "Reckon I better go take the cuffs off the kid? Wouldn't want him to suffer all night, now would we?"

"Yeah, go ahead," I told him. "As soon as I take the horses to the stable, I'm going on home and get to sleep. I didn't get much last night.

~~~~~~

The next morning, just like the one before it came too soon. My dreams were filled with two women fighting over me. And I don't mean with words, them women were punching and kicking and scratching. Never did find out who the winner was, 'cause I woke up.

Harry was still snoring, so I let him sleep on and left without him. I went to Gold's for breakfast. Leslie wasn't very friendly to me. She asked me what I wanted, turned and returned shortly with what I had ordered, slammed it down on the table and left without saying a word.

I finished eating, stood and walked to the front door. I turned as I always did to nod and wave to Leslie, but she had her back to me. I went on outside, stood for a minute,
~~~~~~

then turned toward the little brown house at the end of Faraday Street.

I was already feeling the effects of the newly risen sun or else I was sweating for another reason. I knocked on the door and when it opened I was greeted by someone who I never thought in a million years would be standing in Nora's little house.

You guessed it. I was looking into those hypnotizing green eyes of Rachel.

Talk about being surprised. Lordy, I had to inhale deeply or I do believe I would have passed out from holding my breath.

"Rachel?" my voice squeaked out her name. "What . . . what are you doing here?"

"Don't just stand there, come on in." she grabbed my arm, pulling me inside.

"Good morning, Linc," said Nora as she came in from the kitchen. "How are you this morning?"

"Nora, please, I can explain," I pleaded, looking from her and then to Rachel.

"There's no need for you to explain anything. Rachel and I have talked everything over and have reached a conclusion to the satisfaction of all parties involved."

"You have?" I stammered. "You and Rachel have reached a conclusion?"

"That's correct. You want to tell him, Rachel," she looked at Rachel. "Or shall I?"

"You go ahead, it was your idea," said Rachel.

"Linc," Nora started. "I've felt for some time now that things weren't as they should be between you and me. After all, if two people are engaged to be married, you would assume there would be more of a loving relationship. A mutual agreeing on things of importance. No." she held up her hand when I started to say something. "Let me finish."

She continued talking. "I have felt that you have been growing more distance with each day. I have known and felt your reluctance to get married." She held up her hand again as I opened my mouth. "I'm almost finished. I realize now after discussing things with Rachel why you were acting the way you were. You and I were not meant to be together. I do love you and I always will, but I don't believe I love you the way a wife should love her husband, therefore I am relinquishing any hold that you may feel I have on you and giving it to Rachel. One more thing and I'm finished. I believe that each person has someone out there that is meant to be their mate. A soul mate if you will. I believe with all my heart that Rachel is your soul mate."

I stood there with my mouth hanging open not knowing what to say. I was so worried about what I was going to say to Nora, that I had almost worried myself sick, when all the time everything was being worked out without me having to say a word.

"Close your mouth and kiss me," said Rachel as she put her arms around my neck.

I hesitated, looking at Nora. "Go ahead, enjoy yourself, I've got something to do in the kitchen." She left the room, leaving me and Rachel alone.

Rachel pulled my head down and pressed her lips against mine. It was just like the other time when we kissed in the hotel. Sorry if it sounds like I'm repeating myself, but the moment our lips touched, it was like I was transformed into another world, another realm of reality. Her lips were as soft as smooth velvet, tasted like the sweetest honey ever produced by a swarm of bees. Just as before I could feel the passion building.

I released her lips and stepped back. "If we don't stop now, "I told her. I'm afraid I won't be able to stop."

"I don't want to stop either," she said, keeping her arms around my neck.

"I would suggest you two go see the preacher as soon as possible," said Nora as she came back into the room.

"I don't have anything to wear for a wedding dress," exclaimed Rachel.

"With just some minor adjustments," Nora said. "I believe my dress will fit you perfectly. Come on in here and let's see what we can do. Linc, you go round up the preacher and your best man. I assume you will want Harry."

~~~~~~

Nora is in her realm right now. She really enjoys giving orders to everyone.

"I'm on my way, Nora." I went on the hunt for the preacher and my friend Harry. I found Harry at Gold's
~~~~~~

Eatery enjoying a double helping of flapjacks covered with butter and maple syrup.

"Where you been, partner?" he asked shoveling another big bite into his mouth.

"Finish up, I'm getting married," I told him sitting down on the chair across from him.

"Only question I got," he hesitated, "is which one you marrying?"

"Rachel, of course," with a big grin.

Leslie came over. "Did I overhear something about a wedding, Linc?" she asked.

"Yes, you did, and you're invited," I told her. "In fact, I want to invite the whole town."

"May I ask to whom you are getting married?" she asked with her eyebrows raised. "Nora, I presume?"

"You presume wrong," I said quickly. "Nora has, as she put it, relinquished all rights that she had on me to Rachel. Nora is one fine woman."

"Where you planning on having this wedding inviting the whole town?" asked Leslie.

"I hadn't given it much thought," I told her.

"I don't reckon you have," she said. "Why don't you just invite a few close friends and get married right here."

"You mean here in your place?"

"That's what I'm saying. Business ain't all that good right now, anyhow. I assume you want to get married now," she looked at me, "don't you?"

"Yes," I answered, "right now. As soon as Harry finishes and we find the preacher."

Okay," said Leslie, "you take care of all that stuff. I'll mix up a cake, won't be nothing fancy, but what's a wedding without a cake. Now git moving and I'll take care of things here."

"Thanks, Leslie. Come on Harry, let's find the preacher."

~~~~~~

The wedding went off without a hitch. Of course, there weren't very many folks present. It seems the sheriff doesn't have all that many friends. The wedding dress even with all the adjustments, take-ins and the tucks was still a little big on the bride, but I didn't notice all that. All I saw was my angel standing next to me. The
~~~~~~

cake, just as Leslie had promised wasn't real fancy, but she had decorated it so it was just what was needed.

When the preacher said those words, I now pronounce you husband and wife, I felt like I was on top of the world. He then said, "You may kiss the bride."

I cut the kiss short because I needed to save the passionate one for later.

As soon as everyone congratulated us, we left the Eatery and headed for the hotel.

~~~~~~

"Linc?" Rachel said quietly, so quiet I almost didn't hear.

"Yes?" I looked at her.

"Can we go by the jail," she began twisting her hands together, "and let me see Donnie?"

"Rachel, are you sure you want to do that today, of all days?"

"I need to look him in the eye. I know I told you I wished he was dead, but there were a lot of good times after me and Ma went to live with them. I need to do this, please?"

"If you're sure, then come on."
~~~~~~

We walked through the jail house door and as soon as Donnie saw us he jumped up rushed to the bars and said, "Thank God you're alright. I was worried about you. You left home without saying anything to anybody."

"You know why I left Donnie," she said to him, "and don't say you don't"

"Yeah, I know what Pa was trying to do to you," he said. "I wanted to do something, but I was afraid. You know how mean he could be."

"You wasn't none too nice yourself, Donnie," she looked him in the eye. "How many times did you try something?"

"Aw, Rachel, you ought to know I wouldn't never hurt you. All them times I was just funning with you."

"Well, that's all in the past now," she told him. "I'm starting a new life now. I just got married."

"I'm right proud for you, I wish you a happy life with your new husband."

"Tell me something, Donnie," she asked looking him in the eye again. "Did you do all those things folks are claiming you did? Please tell me the truth."

"Rachel, I swear it wasn't me. I done some bad things, but I ain't never in my whole life killed nobody."

I stepped up and interrupted, "Donnie, I've got a telegram that says you killed a bank teller and president of the bank and an old man as you were riding out of town. Are you saying you didn't do it, when there are eye witnesses?"

"That's what I'm saying," he turned from me and back to Rachel. "You remember Cousin Bart?"

"Yeah," she answered. "I remember him, why?"

"If you remember, him and me, we look enough alike to be brothers. It was him that done all that killing. He's just plain mean clean through. I knowed as soon as I hooked up with him, I done made a mistake, but I needed money. We was gonna just rob the bank and ride outta town. Weren't supposed to be no killing. But like I said, he's just plain mean through and through. Bart shot them folks in cold blood just 'cause they wasn't moving fast enough."

"What about the old man?" I asked. "Witnesses say it was you shot him."

"I was already way down the road. I wanted to git as far away from him as I could. I ain't no killer. I didn't see him shoot nobody, but those two folks in the bank. You know me, Rachel. You believe I could do somethin' like that?"

"You got any idea where this Cousin Bart might be right about now," I asked him.

"I got an idea that he went back to our home place," he said. "Ain't nobody there since pa got hisself killed."

"Okay, Donnie," I said, "if you're telling the truth and we can catch this Bart fellow, will you testify in court everything you've told us just now?"

"I sure will. Am I gonna have to go to prison for robbing that bank and being there when he killed everybody?" he asked, looking at me.

"Let's worry about that when we get this Cousin Bart behind bars."

"You sit tight," Rachel told him. "My new husband will find Bart and bring him back. Don't worry."

~~~~~~

We left the jail and continued our journey toward the hotel.
~~~~~~

"We ain't gonna have no time together yet, are we," she looked up at me and asked.

"I'm truly sorry, darling," I stopped there in the middle of the street and took her hands in mine. "I have to try to bring this fellow to justice."

"I understand," she said with tears forming in her eyes.

"You do your job as sheriff, then come back to me ready to do your duty as a husband," she wiped a tear from her eye.

I gave her a hug and we went to the hotel.

The desk clerk stood as we entered. "I understand congratulations are in order for the new couple. I took the liberty of moving Miss McConnell's, oh excuse me, Mrs. Rhymes' things into a larger room, especially for times like this. The first week is on the house as a wedding present."

I stood there looking at this pimply face greasy haired fellow and wondered if perhaps I had misjudged him. "Thank you for your generosity," I said to him and offered him my hand.

He quickly reached across the desk and took it. "No problem, Sheriff, glad to be of service."

"There is one more thing you could do for me," I still had hold of his hand.

"Of course," he said, trying to pull his hand free.

"Anything, all you have to do is ask." I released his hand.

"Due to unseen circumstances," I told him. "I'm going to have to be out of town for a couple of days. I would appreciate it very much if you would watch out for Mrs. Rhymes, while I'm gone. Do you think you can do that for me?"

"You have to leave now, on your wedding day?" he asked, surprise in in voice.

"Yes," I said. "Unfortunately, the outlaws don't obey all the rules of society like weddings and such."

"I will do my utmost to protect your wife with my life if need be," he snapped to attention and gave me a salute.

"I'll take Mrs. Rhymes to our room if you'll give us the key," I said holding out my hand.

"Oh my, I'm so sorry, all this excitement has affected my brain. Here you are," handing me a key.

On the way to the room, Rachel scolded me, "You know I don't need nobody protecting me. I kin take care of myself. Been doing it for quite a spell, now."

"I know you can, but please humor me," I pleaded with her. "I feel a lot better if there are extra eyes watching out for you."

We reached the room. I inserted the key and turned it.

"Reminds you of the first time we did this, don't it?"

"Sure does," I opened the door. "Only this time is gonna be different." I lifted her in my arms and carried her over the threshold. I stopped just inside the door and stared. The room was huge and had all kinds of fancy stuff in it.

"Well," said Rachel. "You gonna put me down?"

"I let her down and she also took a look around.

"Wow! Is this gonna be our room?" she asked

"It won't be ours until I return, which I better get on the road so I can get back that much sooner." I tilted her head up and kissed her. I felt in that kiss something that I was looking forward to having more of.

"Please be careful, darling," she said as I left.

<div align="center">~~~~~~</div>

I located Harry, filled him in on what we were gonna do. We went to the livery stable to get our mounts.

Albert Hawks, the hostler was standing at the door with our horses saddled ready to go.

"How does he do that?" asked Harry. "Ain't there nothing he don't know?"

"Thanks Albert, much obliged," I told him.

"I took the liberty of putting some victuals in your saddlebags 'cause it's a long trip. You fellers be mighty careful, I hear this one is the worst of the worst. Be best if you shoot first 'afore he does."

"Now, that's some of the best advice I've heard in a long time," Harry agreed.

"We'll be back when we get back," I told Albert. We mounted up and headed out of town.

It was going to take the better part of a full day to reach the McConnell place and we were getting a late start.

"You gonna want to ride straight through?" Harry asked. "Or you wanta look for a place to camp? Oh, never mind, I forgot you're a newly wed."

We pushed the horses, but not really hard. It was close to midnight when we got there. There was a full moon, so we could see the house and yard very clearly.

I pulled on the reins and told Harry, "Hold up!"

The horses stopped while we were a good 150 yards away.

"I sure hope he didn't hear us," said Harry. "We are mighty close, you know."

"Let's work this the same as with Donnie," I told him.

"You work your way around back and I'll wait about five minutes and then ride down there."

"You forgetting something?" he asked.

"What am I forgetting?"

"That ain't Donnie down there. This fellow maybe ain't as green as Donnie. You could be putting yourself in a world of hurt." He said in a pleading voice. "Why don't we try something different?"

"What do you suggest?" I asked him anxious to get this over with.

"Let's both sneak down there, me in the back, you in the front. When one of us hollers, we both bust in front and back doors," he explained. "That should catch him by surprise."

"I knew there was a reason I kept you around," I slapped him on the back. "You gonna holler or you want me to?"

"Well, you are the boss, you do the honors."

"When you gonna quit calling me that? Come on, let's go."

We spread out on both sides of the trail trying to stay as much out of sight as possible. We reached the house without incident. I nodded for Harry to go to the rear and I headed for the front door.

Again, no movement or noise except the beating of my heart. I reached the door, waited, counted to ten and hollered, "NOW!" I lifted my leg and kicked the door almost knocking it off its hinges. I rushed through with my pistol in my hand and saw Harry was in the back door with his weapon drawn.

We both looked around and saw a man lying on a cot in the corner. He looked unconscious. We walked over careful to keep our guns pointed in his direction. The man was barely breathing.

I holstered my weapon and knelt down beside the cot. I placed my finger against the side of his throat. There was a faint pulse. "Get some water, Harry?" I told him.

"Here you go," he handed me a dipper. I poured some on my bandanna and wiped the man's face.

"He started mumbling something. I bent closer and heard him say, "Water? Thirsty. Need water."

I reached behind his head and raised him enough that he could drink from the dipper. He only took a couple little swigs. Then I laid his head back down.

He coughed a couple times, then said, "Donnie didn't do nothing. I done it all, he's innocent of everything. You let him go. He's a good kid that's had a bad growing up." He coughed again and again, then I saw his body relax. His last intake of air was his last. Cousin Bart had left this world and in the process, he left with a cleaner conscious and saved his cousin's life. I pulled the dirty covers up over his face and stood. "See if you can find a shovel, will you Harry?"

~~~~~~

After we had Bart in the ground and said a little prayer for him, we recovered the money from the bank
~~~~~~

robbery, located his horse, leading it behind us as we headed home.

When I let Donnie out of the cell, he said to me, "How come you're letting me go. I told you I took part in the bank robbery."

"I heard you, but I have to take the confession of a dying man over your testimony. Cousin Bart said you were innocent of everything and that includes the robbery. So, you're free to go, but as your new stepbrother in law, let me give you some advice," I put my arm around his shoulder. "Watch who you travel with, stay out of trouble and consider staying right here in town. I'm sure we can find a job for you."

"That sounds like a good plan, but right now I just want to go outside and smell the fresh air." He walked through the door, stopped and took a deep long breath. How anybody could call cow country fresh air is beyond me.

I went back to the hotel, nodded to the clerk, taking the stairs two at a time, rushed down the hallway and raised my hand to knock on the door. It opened before my knuckles touched the wood.

There she stood, "How did you . . . oh heck, it don't make any difference. Come here."

She came into my arms, I lifted her and stepped back across the threshold.

"We already done this part," she teased.

"I just wanted to get it right." I told her and walked across the room laying her on the bed. I lay down beside her turned so I could look into those mesmerizing eyes. I leaned over and our lips touched.

She leaned away from me and said, "I need to say something."

"Okay, what?"

"You remember when you bought me something to eat back when we first met?"

"Of course, I couldn't forget that."

"You remember me wanting to repay you?"

"Yes, I remember."

"That was the first time I had ever done anything like that."

"Are you saying what I think you're saying?"

I've never been with a man, that way. You'll be my first."

"Come here, Sweetheart," wrapping my arms around her.

~~~~~

There is one last thing I need to mention. I don't have to worry about everybody asking (Does Nora Know) anymore, because,

Yes, Nora does know.
~~~~~

Books by J.C. Hulsey

Angel Falls, Texas
Velvet Sky, Arizona
Angry Orchard, Colorado
Clear Stone, Wyoming
Itching Tree, Idaho
Windy Butte, New Mexico
Devil's Dance, Dakota Territory
Redemption Road
Red Rose
Rebecca
The Concho Kid
Ugly Mugly
GUTSHOT
The Last Ride
The Old Man
The Pistol Preacher
Shortland
Dynamite
The Concho Kid
Dead Man's Gun
Does Nora Know
Doke Walker
Brothers
Satan's Refuge
Shadrack
The Brute
The Decision
The Greenhorn
The Gunfight
The Hangman
The Old Timer
Trudy